Spiked Snow

#7

Laban Hill

HYPERION PAPERBACKS FOR CHILDREN

NEW YORK

Printed in the United States

First Edition
1 3 5 7 9 10 8 6 4 2

The text for this book is set in 12-point ACaslon Regular.

ISBN 0-7868-1299-0

Library of Congress Catalog Card Number 98-84826

Photos on insert pages © 1998 by Matt Collins.

XTREME MYSTERIES

#7 Spiked Snow

Speed. Teeth-chattering, bone-shattering, screaming speed. Just duck your head and go!

That's what it's all about.

And that's all Kevin Schultz thought about as he watched the pros stress-test the Winter X Games snow mountain biking racecourse. A deceptive one-mile incline that left your stomach on the starting line and your heart in your throat.

Kevin and his friends—Jamil Smith, Natalie Whittemore, and Walter "Wall" Evans—stood at the icy crest of the run that would be a place of triumph or disaster for the world's top snow mountain bike racers. They were the X-crew, four kids who loved extreme sports and solving mysteries. And they were here to watch the games and have some fun. This was the first games for Nat and Jamil and the first Winter X Games for Kevin and Wall. Kevin and Wall had gone to the Summer X Games in San Diego the year before. That morning

1

Kevin's dad, Gene Schultz, drove them to Crested Butte, Colorado, from their hometown of Hoke Valley, Colorado. Now they were all here to watch their favorite extreme athletes rock the mountain.

The freezing wind of this cold winter afternoon clawed at their cheeks. The falling snow wasn't large and fluffy but small and mean, driving across the mountain sideways in the hard wind.

Jamil looked up at the sky. "Looks like a bad one's coming in." His beanie covered his short blond dreadlocks. At twelve, he was the youngest of the crew. Kevin, Wall, and Nat were all a year older.

Wall nodded. "The snow feels like needles." Right now he was the tallest of the group, but Kevin had been growing at a fierce pace for the last six months and looked to pass him soon.

"This could be disaster for tomorrow's races," Nat added. Today was Wednesday. The games would begin on Thursday.

Nat's long blond ponytail bounced against her neck as she emphasized her point. She was about the same size as Jamil, but while Jamil had a round face with a big crook in his nose where it had been broken a couple of years earlier, Nat's face was pointy in a way that most people would say was beautiful.

The wind picked up, but it didn't seem to know which direction it wanted to go. Instead, the air on the butte swirled this way and that. Still, its force kept increasing and the snow stung even more. Everyone pulled up their scarves over their faces.

"Weather is just one more obstacle," Jeff Fahey interrupted. He had just arrived at the crest on a caterpillar after his last practice run. "And that's what I love about it. It's way radical to head down a hill and not be sure how it's going to end." He smiled underneath his fleece mask.

Jeff was the gnarliest snow mountain bike racer on the hill. The crew had met him earlier when Jason Korm introduced them. Jason owned Ultimate Sports in Crested Butte, and was a friend of Kevin's dad, who owned a sporting goods store in Hoke Valley. Jason had invited Mr. Schultz, Kevin, and his friends to stay with him during the games.

"The burlier the mountain, the larger you have to go!" Jeff continued as he pulled his bike off the cat. He lifted his bike over his head and yelled up to the sky. "You're not going to stop me!" He was practicing on the course for Saturday's races.

Nat smiled. Mountain biking was her favorite extreme sport. And she was ready to ride in any kind of weather, too. She loved racing in the rain, but she and her friends had never raced on snow. "I just hope I get a chance to try the course," she said to no one in particular.

Just then the starting bell rang and Jill Sumter, one of the competitors in the women's downhill, shot out of the gate and wailed down the mountain. She wore a bright-orange skintight rubberized suit like nearly every other racer on the mountain that afternoon. These suits were

specially made to cut down on wind resistance.

"Next!" Kevin shouted, like he was waiting for his turn to play a schoolyard game. He was just as good a mountain biker as Nat, but he was also good at everything. He was one of those kids who could try a sport for the first time and beat everyone else at it. He had an amazing ability to break down technique to its basic movements and then recreate them after watching someone else only once.

Wall snorted. "What're you going to ride? This is the X Games, dude. Not some backyard ski slope." Wall pulled his knit beanie down on his head. Even though he loved the cold, having spent most of his life in the mountain wilderness with a dad who was an avalanche expert, the weather was definitely bothering him.

"Well, you can always dream," Kevin replied. "The only thing I want to do this weekend is try snow mountain biking and meet Chase Johnson." Chase Johnson was the most radical half pipe rider at the games. Kevin looked to see if there was an extra bike lying around. He was determined to give this course a try.

"Don't worry, Kev. You got next," Jason called as he hopped off the cat. "My old roomie Jeff will be happy to lend you his bike." Jason slapped Jeff on the back. They had gone to college in Vermont together and had remained friends ever since.

"I can't borrow Jeff's bike. What if I crash?" Kevin protested. He definitely didn't want to be responsible for Jeff's bike if he chundered.

"It's not his bike," Jason explained. "It's a loner from my store so Jeff doesn't risk breaking his own before tomorrow's race."

"What?" Jeff replied. Dressed in a Day-Glo green skin suit, he held the small, undersized bike against his thigh. "Just as long as I don't have to lend him my skin suit and fairings." Unlike last year, just about every competitor was wearing one of these skin suits now, and some had leg fairings strapped to their calves. Leg fairings were wedge-shaped sections of rubberized, lycra-covered Styrofoam that were attached to the calves in order to cut down on turbulence. Snow mountain biking was so new that at just about every event the technology changed in some major way. The raging discussion at this games was whether to use knobbies or flat treads on tires. Everybody had an opinion. Jeff had opted for flat treads, believing that knobbies slowed the tires down in the snow. "Do you think he can handle it?"

"What are you saying? The guy who was nicknamed Maniac is worried that it might be dangerous?" Jason cracked. "The guy who rode his bike off the roof of our dorm into a pile of fresh powder is thinking safety first?" He paused. "My boy's getting old." He patted Jeff on the back.

Jeff shrugged. "Things have changed over the last five years since we graduated. I could have broken my neck back then. I didn't even wear a helmet." Jeff tore off his chest protector, elbow pads, and knee pads, and tossed them to Kevin. "You better wear these." Then he bent over and picked up his helmet, which looked like something out of a 1950s sci-fi movie. Its sides swooped out to cover the space between the head and shoulders. It also had a Plexiglas visor over the front opening.

Kevin dropped to the snow and strapped on the protective gear. "Velcro. What did the world do before Velcro?"

"Broke their bones!" Jamil cracked.

"Stoked and ready!" Kevin shouted as he got up and straddled the bike. "Hey, this bike is too small!" Kevin noticed for the first time that the bike had only a twelve-inch frame. He was expecting a normal eighteen-inch frame. "You must be a foot taller than I am. How do you ride this?" He lifted to front wheel off the ground by the handlebars.

Jeff laughed. "You want to stay close to the ground when you're on snow and ice. The higher up you are the less control you have." Jeff crouched like he was riding an invisible bike. "Remember to keep low."

Kevin nodded and waited for the starting bell to announce that the course was clear. A fine spray of snow collected on his visor, melting so that beads of water covered the Plexiglas. It seem like he was looking at the slope through a fish tank.

After a few seconds, the bell rang loudly.

Kevin awkwardly started the bike forward and began to peddle. The bike's small size made it feel like he was riding his little sister's bike back home.

But it didn't take long for Kevin to start picking up

speed. Ten yards down the slope Kevin's rear wheel spun out to the left as he tried to make the first turn. He leaned over his handlebars and jerked the bike back under his body. He squeezed the front brake, locking the tire. In the blink of an eye he was sailing over the handlebars in a classic endo. He tumbled a couple of times end over end down the course.

"Nice facial!" Nat shouted. "A perfect addition for a Classic Wipeouts video."

Everyone laughed, but Kevin knew his friends were just goofing on him.

Kevin waved to show that he was all right. His cheek had a bright-red strawberry on it and he was covered head to toe with snow, but nothing was broken.

"This is harder than it looks," he huffed as he carried the bike up the slope.

"Your first frozen corn dog!" Jamil said. "Instead of dust, you're wrapped in snow."

"Ha ha," Kevin said, brushing himself off.

"You braked too hard," Jeff explained. "Your bike fishtailed on that icy patch." He pointed to a bare spot in the middle of the slope. "Then when you braked, the front tire bit into the corn snow after the ice and locked up. You have to trust that you're not going to fall, and not brake too hard or quickly. The bike will stay under you if you don't overcorrect."

Kevin nodded as Wall knelt beside the bike and examined the tires.

"These tires are totally rad," Wall exclaimed. "The

smooth street tread makes the tires almost like a snow-board, especially since they're so wide. How wide are they? Two and half inches? How do they work on the snow?"

Jeff smiled like he was impressed with Wall's question. "They really cut down on turbulence. Knobby tires slow you down. And as I always say, if you trust them, they will work."

Kevin could tell Jeff was totally into Wall's question. Jeff grabbed the bike from Kevin and flipped it over. He spun the wheel. "With a snowboard or a ski, the friction against the slope melts the snow so that there's actually a thin film of water between the board and the snow. The way I figure it, a smooth street tread will do the same thing while the studs anchor you in the snow."

"Awesome," Wall replied.

"This is all really interesting, guys," said Kevin. "But right now I'm more interested in redeeming myself on those tires, not talking about them."

Jeff set the bike back on its tires and gave it to Kevin.

"We'll grab the cat and meet you at the bottom," Jeff said. "It's getting too hairy up here, so yours will be one of the last runs today."

"All right," said Kevin. "I'll see you in a few."

Jeff, Jason, Nat, Jamil, and Wall climbed on the back of the caterpillar and rode down the slope.

"I promised Kevin's dad we'd meet him at the store in an hour," Jason said. Mr. Schultz had hit the slopes to get some skiing in. He was a major ski bum.

In the gate, Kevin decided to come out more cautiously and then pick up speed when he was certain he was in control. As he waited for the bell, the falling snow got thicker. He couldn't see more than a dozen feet ahead. He considered bailing on the run for a moment, but the thought of losing his chance to snow mountain bike at the X Games quickly outweighed his fears. Even if it was just a practice run before the games really started, it was still the X Games.

For a second he imagined Missy Giove, the X Games reporter, standing at the bottom of the slope with a mike in her hand, speaking to the television audience. "Kevin Schultz is about to make his second run and he's in medal contention."

A few seconds later the bell rang again. Kevin threw his chest forward and cranked the right pedal while his left foot dragged along the snow. He left the gate much slower this time. He used his feet to keep his balance and let his momentum carry him down. Snow kicked up behind him in a shallow tail.

"All right," said Kevin. "I'll see you in a few."

After about twenty-five yards Kevin's feet hit the flat pedals hard and fast. He cranked it coming into the first turn. He could feel the bike slipping out from under him again, but this time he dabbed the snow with his inside foot, and kept control. The bike chattered across a washboard straightaway and Kevin hung on for life. His feet bounced on the flatties. This caused excessive cranial disharmony.

The next turn came off a radical berm but the dual suspension bike just swallowed up the bump. *Boing-boing.*

As Kevin hit the half mile mark, he felt like he was about to bonk, but he ground his teeth and tucked his head. His muscles tensed as if his life depended on them. And it did. If he fell now, he'd have a serious chance discovering he really wasn't Gumby.

One more turn and the final straightaway to go—a long icy hill that had a couple of dangerous bumps. He leaned into the turn, treating the snow like it was mud. Luckily, the studs held on the frozen surface. He hit the straightaway going at a burly clip.

The bike flew over the first bump. Kevin thought he was going to fly off, but he held on. The second bump was easier, but he still caught more air than he wanted. But he managed to land firmly on his tires without a waver.

Kevin knew he was home free now, so he leaned back and enjoyed the ride. The bike hurled down the steep slope and Kevin simply hung on.

"Yeeeyow!" Kevin yelled. But his excitement quickly drained when he realized that he was going to have to stop. Kevin dragged his feet and lightly flexed the brakes so the tires wouldn't lock up.

He came to a stop just in front of the crash pad. Kevin tore off his helmet. He couldn't believe he'd made it all the way down.

A couple of minutes later the rest of the group arrived.

"Great run, Kev," Jeff said.

"Yeah, Kevin, that rocked!" Jason added. He picked up the bike and slung it on his shoulder. "We better get back to the store." Then Jason turned to Nat, Wall, and Jamil. "Don't panic. You guys will get a chance after the competition ends. They're planning on keeping the course in place for a couple of days after the games."

"I can dig that," Jamil replied.

"Let's go," Kevin suggested. He was now totally charged from the ride. "Dad said you have an awesome climbing wall."

"That's right," Jason answered. "You've got to try it. I hear you're quite the climber. You're even teaching now." They headed around the side of the ski lodge and toward the shuttle that would take them downtown. The marketplace was on Elk Avenue. Hotels, restaurants, and stores flanked the street for about half a mile, then spilled out into a municipal parking lot. Ultimate Sports was on this strip about halfway down.

On Elk Avenue the group snaked through the crowds of vacationers who had come to see the games. The energy in the air was electric.

Nat came up beside Jason. "Kev said we're going to stay in the store."

"I thought you guys would enjoy that better than my tiny condo," Jason explained. "Kev's dad and I are about all that can fit."

11

"Awesome!" Wall said. He could deal with endless wall time.

"This is going to be the best X Games ever!" Kevin exclaimed.

"Cold!" Nat grumbled the next morning.

Kevin woke with a start. Nat was already standing. Her arms wrapped around her body, trying to keep the heat in. She was wearing sweat pants and a sweatshirt with a beanie pulled down on her head. "Do you think Jason would mind if we turned on the heat?"

Kevin slid out of his down sleeping bag. He only had on a pair of shorts and a T-shirt. "Is it cold? I didn't notice."

Nat narrowed her eyes and smiled. "What? You don't get cold?"

"I'm specially trained to withstand the elements," Kevin joked.

"Yeah, right," Jamil cut in. He was out of his sleeping bag and already rolling it up. "The last time we went winter camping all you did was complain about how cold it was."

13

"I wasn't complaining," Kevin replied. "I was just making an observation."

"You're such a liar," Nat said. She wrapped her sleeping bag around herself like a cloak.

"Anybody know what time it is?" Wall asked with a yawn. He buried himself deeper into his bag.

"Must be early. It's still dark," Jamil answered.

"I don't think so," Nat countered. She went to the front of the store where a strange, shallow white light came through the front window. "It's not dark. The window is covered in snow!"

The window that spanned the entire front of the store was blocked by a huge pile of snow.

The other kids hurried to Nat's side.

"I hope nobody's claustrophobic!" Nat cracked.

"What's claustro . . . whatever?" Jamil asked.

"Afraid of enclosed spaces," Nat answered.

Wall suddenly began to tremble. "Uh, guys, I am." His breath became quick and he grabbed his throat. "I can't catch my breath."

Jamil started to panic. "What do we do?"

Wall burst out laughing.

"Let's lock him in the closet," Jamil said.

Wall settled down. "Thanks for the support, dude."

"You're so funny I forgot to laugh," Jamil said sarcastically. He looked over at the window to change the subject. "The weatherman really got it wrong last night. They said it wasn't supposed to snow that much."

"I just hope it's not still snowing," Wall said as he put

his hand against the frozen glass door. "I feel like I'm living in an igloo."

"Is there a back door or some other way out of here?" Nat asked.

Kevin shook his head. "We better call Jason. Maybe he can dig us out." He picked up the phone by the cash register but it was dead. "The snow must have knocked out the phones."

Jamil pulled at the collar of his T-shirt. "Do you think we could suffocate in here?" he asked nervously. He wasn't joking.

"Not a chance," Wall answered. "This store isn't a sealed environment like a refrigerator or a safe. We'll have plenty of air."

Jamil smiled with relief. "I just hope you're right this time." He paused. "But what if this is the beginning of the next ice age? What if the entire earth has been covered with snow?"

"Then it's been nice knowing you," Wall cracked.

"Well, what do we do now?" Nat asked.

"Nothing we can do but wait," Kevin answered.

"What about breakfast?" Nat asked. "I'm getting hungry."

Jamil dug in a box on the desk. "Sports bars!" He tore open a bar and chomped.

"Cool!" Wall said as he snagged one.

"We're going to have to pay for these," Kevin warned his friends.

"I know," Jamil said. "But it's not our fault we're

buried alive. Do you want us to starve to death?"

"Especially when the alternative is to start eating each other," Nat replied. She bit into a bar and smiled. "You guys would taste nasty."

"No way," Jamil responded. "Being the youngest, I'd be the tenderest, like a filet mignon. You old folks would be tough and tasteless."

"Can the morbid stuff," Kevin cut in. "What should we do? Try to dig out?"

"The doors push out," Wall reminded him. "We'll never by able to open them with all that snow piled against them."

Kevin nodded. "Then what?"

Jamil tore open two bars at one time.

"Hey! Don't be a hog," Nat shouted at him. "What if we're buried for days? We need to ration these." She closed the box of bars and held on to them tightly so no one else could have more.

Jamil shrugged. "Hwa bbbuu mmummm . . ."

"Didn't your parents teach you any manners?" Nat said, disgusted. "Don't talk with your mouth full."

Jamil swallowed hard. "What I was trying to say is, I'm sure someone will be here soon to dig us out. So in the meantime, why don't we check out the climbing wall?"

The crew went straight for the climbing gear.

"I got first," Jamil shouted. He grabbed a harness and started adjusting it to fit.

"Hey! Do you hear that?" Wall shouted.

A muffled growl filled the air.

"The monster is waking," Jamil said.

Nat waved Jamil off and she ran to the window. "No, someone's digging us out."

The crew hurried over.

The faint light filtering through the snow brightened. Then they saw the edge of a shovel. Suddenly a hole appeared and through the hole . . .

"Dad!" Kevin shouted. Mr. Schultz peered into the store. Kevin rapped his knuckles on the window. His dad smiled.

Ten minutes later the entrance was cleared.

Jamil staggered out. "Water . . . water . . . I need water."

"Here's some water," Nat said as she scooped up some snow and threw it in Jamil's face.

Jamil smiled and packed a snowball with his bare hands. As he wound up to nail Nat, he got hit on the back the head. Jamil turned. Wall stood about ten feet away laughing. Jamil chucked his snowball.

Wall ducked. "Too slow!"

Before anything else could be sorted out, the crew

was in a full-blown snowball fight. Kevin's dad and Jason quickly took refuge in the store. The only thing that stopped the battle was that everyone's hands got too cold.

It was nearly an hour before the snowplow had completely cleared the snow.

Inside the store, the crew was bubbling with questions.

"Is the whole town buried?" Kevin asked.

"Are the games postponed?" Nat asked.

"There must have been some wicked winds," Wall said.

"Yeah," Jamil said. "I'm surprised they didn't wake us up."

Jason held up his hands. "One question at a time. First of all, this snow didn't come from a storm. Someone pushed the piles of snow that were along the curb against the store's front window."

"You better be glad the window didn't break," Mr. Schultz commented.

"But who?" Kevin asked.

"And why?" Nat asked.

The crew was beginning to sniff out a mystery and that always got them excited.

"It's probably just a prank," Jason said dismissively. "Don't worry about it."

Kevin, Nat, Jamil, and Wall gave each other a funny look. Why didn't Jason seem concerned?

"But your store is opening two hours late," Kevin said. "That's a lot of missed customers on a big weekend like this."

"It's not going to make or break me," Jason replied.

"What do you know?" Kevin pressed. "You must know who did it if you're not mad."

Jason smiled. "Your dad said that you guys were crack detectives. You're right. I think I know who did this."

"Who?" they all asked at once.

"Jeff. This is just the kind of stunt he'd pull off in college," Jason explained. "I remember when he collected all the Christmas trees from the neighborhood after New Year's and piled them in our room."

"That's wild," Jamil exclaimed.

"He's a maniac. He'd do anything to shock me," Jason continued. He turned on the register and the lights in the store. Mr. Schultz went into the back to make coffee.

Kevin waved his friends over to the climbing wall. "I'm not so sure Jeff would do this. This seems a little extreme to me."

"But hey! This is the X Games!" Jamil countered.

"Still, this seems like a lot of trouble to go to for a joke," Kevin argued. "How did he find a snowplow? He doesn't live here. Whose plow did he borrow?"

Wall yelled across the store, "Hey, Jason. Does Jeff have a snowplow?"

Jason smiled. "His sports utility vehicle is rigged for one, but the short answer is no. He didn't come with one on his SUV as far as I know. But he could have easily hooked a plow up to do his dirty work last night." He went into the back.

Nat shrugged. "That seems like a lot of trouble."

"Should we investigate?" Wall asked his friends.

"I vote yes," Kevin replied.

Jamil and Nat nodded.

"This shouldn't take long," Nat added. "Jeff will probably confess when we confront him."

"That's true," Kevin admitted. "If it's him. But I'm not so sure."

Jamil glanced at the clock over the counter. It read eleven o'clock. "Hey! The games started an hour ago! Jeff doesn't compete until later this afternoon, but I want to catch some other stuff."

"I say we wait until after he competes to talk to him," Nat suggested. "I doubt he'll want to talk to us about the weather before the race, much less sabotage."

"Good point," agreed Kevin. "I doubt anything more will happen during the day, and he might be a lot less agreeable when he's nervous even if he didn't do anything."

"So let's ride now," Wall suggested. "We can catch some of the races on our way down the mountain."

"Good thinking," Nat said. "I think I'd go nuts if I just sat around all day watching someone else have all the fun."

"Let's jet," Kevin said. "The practice runs on the pipe should be happening now. I want to see if Chase is there." Chase Johnson was Kevin's snowboarding idol. Kevin's games would be made if he could shake Chase's hand and say hi.

The crew got dressed and grabbed their snowboards. They headed out the door, but were stopped by a man

running toward Ultimate Sports. Ignoring the kids, he barged straight past them and into the store.

"I guess he's got to get that new snowboard now," Jamil cracked.

"We better find out what is going on," Kevin suggested. "He looked really upset. Maybe it has something to do with the store being buried." They went back in the store.

"Rico, calm down and tell me what's wrong," they heard Jason saying as they walked in.

"My restaurant was plowed in last night just like your store," the man exclaimed.

The crew looked at each other in surprise.

"This doesn't sound like a joke between college roommates anymore," Kevin said.

"We definitely better investigate," Wall said.

"Someone piled snow in front of my restaurant the same as your store," the man explained to Jason.

Anger crossed Jason's face as he listened. "I'm going to kill Jeff. It's one thing to play a joke on me, but it goes beyond a game when he pulls stunts on other businesses."

"Which restaurant do you own?" Kevin interrupted.

"La Strada, an Italian restaurant," the man replied.

"I'm sorry. I forgot to introduce you," Jason apologized. "This is Rico Allesandro." Mr. Allesandro shook Kevin's hand. "And these are some friends who are up for the games; Gene, his son, Kevin, and Kevin's friends Nat, Wall, and Jamil."

Nat, Wall, and Jamil nodded. Mr. Schultz gave a small wave as he stepped outside.

"Have you cleared the snow away yet?" Nat asked.

Mr. Allesandro shook his head. "The plow is on the way."

Nat turned to her friends. "We better get over there fast."

"Yeah, before any clues are destroyed," Wall added.

"Where's your restaurant?" Kevin asked.

"Down the street about three blocks," Mr. Allesandro said as he pointed.

The crew left their snowboards in Jason's office and took off.

It wasn't hard to figure out which place it was. They just had to find the restaurant that looked like it had been buried in an avalanche.

The crew got there just in time. The trucks had arrived, but the drivers were waiting for Mr. Allesandro. They stood beside the massive dump truck with three plows attached to the front—one shovel in the front and one on each side of that one. The shovels could be directed depending on where the driver wanted to push the snow. A small Bobcat front loader stood nearby to load the snow into the dump truck.

"Where's Rico?" the plow driver asked.

"He'll be here in a minute," Kevin answered as he passed the drivers.

"We better see if we can find any tire treads," Wall suggested.

The crew examined the street.

"We probably won't find the perp's footprints," Nat commented. "since he probably didn't get out of his vehicle."

"However," Kevin continued her thought, "it's clear

which tire track belongs to the vehicle that did this because there's only one leading to the snow bank."

"We better get a photo of this and measure it while we're at it," Nat said.

"I've got a camera back at the store and I'll ask Jason for a ruler," Nat said as she turned down the street. The rest of the gang stood in a circle around the tire track to protect it.

Nat returned in a matter of minutes. She loaded her camera with film and took about ten pictures from all different angles. Then she took pictures of the entire snow pile. "Let's find a one-hour photo place and get this roll developed," Nat said when she had finished.

At that moment, Mr. Allesandro returned with Jason and Mr. Schultz. Mr. Allesandro directed the snow to be removed. "My restaurant is to open in an hour and I haven't prepared anything." He looked really upset. "One of the biggest weekends of the year and I'm going to lose my lunch business." He sat on a bench and shook his head in disgust.

Jason's jaw was locked in anger. "This time Jeff's gone too far, but right now I have to open the store. I'll talk to him later." He marched down the street.

"I hope for Jeff's sake he didn't do it," Jamil said, watching Jason storm away.

"I don't think he did," Kevin replied. "But I don't think that will matter to Jason. He's going to take Jeff's head off no matter what."

"You're certainly right about that," agreed Mr.

Schultz. "So I'm going to go back to the store to give Jason a hand, and to see if I can calm him down a bit. Even if Jeff did do all this, Jason's only going to make matters worse by getting so angry about it. I'll see you kids later."

"Bye, Dad," Kevin said.

Mr. Schultz turned back toward the store.

"I still say we stick to our plan to talk to Jeff later," Nat said. "In the meantime we can get the pictures developed." Nat took the roll of film out of the camera. "Excuse me, Mr. Allesandro, but do you know where we could get a roll of film developed?"

"There's a photo place in the Crested Butte Regent Hotel." He pointed back down Elk Avenue. "It's down that way. You can't miss it."

"Thanks," Nat said. She led her friends on their first step to solving this mystery.

As the crew hurried away, they spotted a police cruiser with its lights flashing just ahead. Two police officers were escorting a man into the car. The man did not look very happy about this. The trunk of the cruiser was open and a pile of T-shirts and souvenirs were stacked inside.

"Looks like he's getting busted," Jamil commented. He slowed to watch the scene.

"That's one mystery that doesn't need solving," Nat cracked. "Let's go!" She grabbed his sleeve and pulled him along.

At the photo store, Nat handed the film to the clerk.

"We need the pictures in an hour."

The clerk laughed. "Not a chance. With the games happening everyone is taking pictures like crazy. And I'm the only one here today."

Kevin groaned. He knew what that meant.

"You'll have to give me three or four hours," the clerk replied. "Better yet, could you pick it up tomorrow morning?"

Nat shook her head. "This is a rush. Your sign says one hour."

The clerk handed the roll of film back to Nat. "I'm sorry but I'm just too busy."

Nat refused to take the film. "All right, three hours. We'll be back in three hours." She gave the guy her name, and they headed back to Ultimate Sports to pick up their snowboards.

Elk Avenue was fairly empty. Most everyone in town was on the mountain. By the time they reached the store, Jason was much calmer. He and Mr. Schultz were preparing to work out on the climbing wall. Mr. Schultz was about to start climbing. Jason was working the belay.

"Hey, Dad, knock yourself out," Kevin called.

Mr. Schultz waved.

"You kids heading to the slopes?" Jason asked.

Kevin nodded. "We've got a lot planned." He smiled, knowing that he meant more than just the games. "We're going to catch the shuttle now."

Just then, a man with long gray hair pulled back in a ponytail bumbled into the store. He was wearing an old

27

blanket stadium jacket with worn leather buttons. In his arms was a large folder with papers spilling out.

At first Kevin thought he was lost, but Jason seemed to know him.

As the old man bent to pick up the papers, he called to Jason, "Do you have a minute? I want to give you a petition to halt further development in town. It's got a hundred signatures on it already."

Jason turned to Mr. Schultz. "Sorry, Gene, duty calls." He let the rope slip through the belay. "What's up, Scott?"

Scott set his folder down on the counter and starting sorting through it. "I have a hundred names," he repeated. As he sorted through the papers he found a piece of hard candy stuck to a page. "Hmmm." He peeled it off and popped it into his mouth.

Kevin, Nat, Jamil, and Wall looked at each other and tried not to laugh.

"This guy is strange," Jamil whispered.

Nat socked him in the arm to shut him up. They stood by the door and watched the scene unfold.

"Why don't you drop the petition off at next week's Chamber of Commerce meeting?" Jason suggested.

Scott waved his hand dimissively. "No. No. I have it right here. You're the chair of the subcommittee on the games, so you're supposed to get this before the meeting." He dug through the papers for a couple more minutes.

The X-crew watched him silently.

Scott muttered to himself. Then he stacked the

March's cruisin'!

Snow Mountain Bike Racer Shaums March

Although Shaums March moved many times as a child, he always remembers being outside in the snow and the mountains. When Shaums was eighteen years old, he decided to start mountain biking. He entered his first race when he and his friend dared each other into competing, and although he placed last, the race pushed him to improve. In his first season, Shaums quickly went from Beginner, to Sport, to Expert Class, and in 1996, he went Pro.

ESPN's X Games offer Shaums and other dirt mountain bikers another way to compete—snow mountain biking. In 1997, Shaums participated in his first X Games. In 1998, he designed the Downhill and Dual Slalom courses for the Winter X Games and placed fourth in the Dual Slalom competition! Shaums lives in Santa Barbara,CA but spends most of his time on the road participating in various competitions.

MARCH'S SNOW MOUNTAIN BIKING
SAFETY TIPS

Wear protective gear at all times.
Ride within your ability.
Try to ride with others, rather than alone.
Don't do drugs.

March at age 9

Age: 24

Most memorable competition: Gotta Thunder, 1995. This is a two-day race with two different courses and two different runs. I beat two of the top pros while I was only in the Expert class.

Favorite athlete: I never really had one; I was too busy playing outside!

Favorite bike: Ellsworth Handcrafted Bicycles

What I like best about my sport: Being around all the people that love riding as much as I do.

Favorite thing to do on a Saturday: Wake up late, relax in bed, listen to music, and pretend that I have nothing to do.

Favorite pig-out food: Sushi and pizza

Favorite movie: *Rad* (BMX movie)

papers back in the folder. With an embarrassed smile, he said, "I must have left it at the office."

Jason nodded. "It's all right, Scott. I'll make sure it gets on the agenda. Just bring the petition to the meeting."

"Thanks, Jason," Scott replied. "See you next week." He put on a pair of brown earmuffs and left.

"What a character," Mr. Schultz commented. He still stood by the wall with the rope tied to his carbiner.

Jason laughed. "Scott English is a little strange, but he's a brilliant lawyer, one of the toughest to go against. He almost single-handedly stopped the X Games from coming to Crested Butte."

"Why?" Wall asked.

"He's antidevelopment. He's afraid any growth will harm the mountain environment," Jason explained. "One good thing about his fight has been that we've had to make sure the ecosystem is not destroyed. We've ended up putting in all kinds of safeguards to protect the mountain." Jason slipped the rope back into his belay.

"Well, we're out like trout," Jamil said.

"See you kids later," Mr. Schultz said.

"Catch up with you tonight, Dad," Kevin replied as he and his friends picked up their boards and headed out of the store.

"I'll probably see you at the snow mountain bike races this afternoon," Jason called after them. Then he scowled. "Jeff and I have a lot to discuss."

The X-crew walked a block to the shuttle.

"Let's ride and then catch the snow mountain bike

dual downhill," Wall suggested as they climbed on the bus.

"Maybe we'll be able to talk to Jeff at the race," Jamil replied. "If he's the perp, we can wrap up this case before the end of the first day of the games."

"Jason seems to think he is," Jamil said.

"And if not, it'll be about time to pick up the photos," Nat reminded everyone. "But Jason could be wrong. Until Jeff actually says he did it, we need to keep an open mind."

"I'm with you, Nat," Wall added. "I remember when we jumped to conclusions a couple of months ago. We almost got the new skateboard park closed down before it was even built."

Everyone agreed. That mystery had been a really tough one. They were all surprised when they discovered who the real culprit was.

"That's a good reminder not to get ahead of our evidence," Kevin said.

The shuttle stopped in the parking lot of the ski slope. Signs and banners were plastered everywhere, either advertising sponsors of the games or directing spectators where to go for the different competitions. Crowds poured in and out of the lodge. The lift lines seemed endless.

When Kevin saw the lines, he decided not to waste his time there. "I'm heading to the snow boarding half pipe. Maybe Chase will be there," Kevin said.

"Catch you later," Jamil said. "I'm dying to ride that

double black diamond run that everybody raves about."

"I'm with you, Jamil," Wall said.

"Me, too," Nat added.

Kevin split off from his friends and headed for the terrain park.

Water freezes at 32 degrees Fahrenheit. Snow is perfect at 18 degrees Fahrenheit. When it reaches −5 degrees, it's too cold. The snow becomes hard and granular like sand. Riding on this kind of snow is like sliding on a sand dune. On the mountain at Crested Butte the conditions were nearly perfect—ten degrees with packed powder as light as air.

Kevin scooped up a handful of the powder and blew it into the air. For a moment the cloud of snow hung there. Then it drifted like thousands of tiny, weightless feathers to the ground. This kind of snow wouldn't hold together to make a snowball or a snowman, but it made him want to strap on his board in the worst way. He carried it with him as he climbed the slope to the snowboard park. There the half pipe was carved out of the mountain.

Kevin could hear the music blasting before he could

see the pipe. He recognized the band. It was a rockin' indie band named The Four Color Manual.

But Kevin wasn't paying much attention to the music. In the back of his mind something was off about this mystery. He could almost understand Jeff plowing in Jason's store, but why would he also plow in Mr. Allesandro's restaurant? He had no reason to. Kevin's gut told him this wasn't going to end this afternoon when they talked to Jeff.

Walking uphill in snow wearing snowboarding boots was not exactly easy. Kevin was also carrying his snowboard under his arm. By the time he reached the bottom of the pipe he was winded. He sucked air with short, shallow breaths that made his heart race. He dropped his board and found a spot on the edge of the pipe. Concentrating on taking long, deep breaths, he scanned the line of a dozen or so boarders, both pros and amateurs, waiting to drop in. He hoped Chase Johnson was among them.

Kevin smiled when he finally spotted Chase, who was next up.

Along the edge of the pipe a crowd of riders sat or stood as they cheered a rider's McTwist. The rider who was in the pipe now was not anyone that Kevin recognized, but she sure rode like a pro. She boned a monster invert and then followed that with an Indy Air. Her red hair fluttered behind her like a flag as she crossed the pipe's flat bottom. She ended her run with a stylin' Pop Tart.

Kevin watched her climb out of the pipe and sit next to him. He nodded and she nodded back.

The sun broke through the clouds and quickly heated things up. Sweat beaded in Kevin's afro and ran down the side of his face. It always amazed Kevin that he could sweat when it was ten degrees outside. He unzipped his parka and wiped his face off with his light-blue wool scarf. He was glad his inner layer of clothes would wick the sweat away from his body.

At the edge of the pipe Chase strapped his back foot onto his board and slid into position.

"Rock it, Chase!" the red-haired girl yelled.

Chase waved to her. Then he pulled his goggles over his face and threw his shoulders forward. His board followed. He whipped down the side of the pipe into the well and up the opposite side.

Riding the half pipe was a lot like being on a roller coaster—just without the screaming. A half pipe is the perfect shape for translating vertical speed into horizontal speed. Just like a coaster's monster curves, the half pipe slingshots the rider while losing only the smallest amount of speed.

Chase rode up the opposite side and shot a couple of feet above the lip in a simple transfer. His speed increased on the next pass and he boned out a super-good method at least five feet above the lip.

"Sick!" shouted Kevin.

The crowd cheered. No one expected Chase to do such a rad trick so early in the pipe. Most riders need at least two more passes before they have the momentum to go that big.

Chase, on the other hand, was just beginning his ride. And that was what made him so awesome. He came up the backside of the pipe and pounded his hands into the coping for a burly Ho-Ho.

Yeah's bubbled through the crowd.

Unlike other riders who sometimes looked like they were struggling just to keep their balance, Chase never let a trick get in the way of building more speed. He used his hands to push off hard as he landed fakie and shot down the side.

This was his fourth pass across the flat bottom. If he worked it right, he could squeeze out five more passes.

Chase came up the frontside wall riding fakie and in perfect position to huck some sort of Cab. He came out of the pipe and began to spin. But when he reached 180 degrees, he froze in midair and rewound the trick to land in the same spot fakie.

Kevin went wild. He threw his fist into the air and leaped to his feet. No one had ever done that before.

"If he sticks that trick in the competition, nobody's going to beat him," the red-haired girl next to Kevin gasped.

"It ruled!" Kevin said. "Chase is my boy. He's like a god."

The girl smiled. "You want to meet him?"

Stunned, Kevin stammered, "You've got to be kidding. Of course I want to meet him."

"I'll introduce you," she said. "I'm Gail."

"Hi, I'm Kevin."

Kevin and the girl turned back to the pipe. Chase was coming back up the frontside wall after he had pulled off a Stale Egg. He had used up a lot of territory on the pipe on the last two passes. This was going to be his last trick and that meant he would go large.

Chase crouched as he rose into the air and spun clockwise. When he reached about 360 degrees, he threw his head down between his legs and performed a front flip that finished off with another 180 degrees.

"Awesome McTwist," Kevin said.

But Chase didn't quite stick it. He overrotated and landed on his can. He slid down to the end of the pipe where the girl Kevin had spoken to now was.

Kevin scooted down to them. He wasn't about to let shyness get in the way of his chance to meet Chase Johnson. A huge grin was plastered on his face as he held his hand out to Chase, who was still sitting on the snow.

Chase grabbed it and used it to pull himself up. "Thanks, dude."

"Very fresh ride," Kevin said.

"Thanks, man," Chase said.

"This is Kevin," Gail interrupted. "Kevin, this is Chase."

Chase shook Kevin's hand again. "You ride?"

"Every moment I can grab," Kevin replied.

"Cool. I'm through for the day, but if you're around after the competition tomorrow, I'll be free to give you some tips," Chase volunteered as he unstrapped his feet.

Gail brushed snow off Chase's back.

"Really? You're not lying?" Kevin said excitedly.

"Not a chance." Chase glanced up the pipe. "Why don't you practice and we'll talk tomorrow, dude."

"I'm totally stoked," Kevin replied. "Are you going to the party tonight?"

"Wouldn't miss it."

"Well, I'm hoping to be there, too," Kevin said. "So maybe I'll see you later."

"Yeah, sure. Nice meeting you." Chase picked up his board and walked off with Gail.

Kevin climbed the slope to the top of the pipe and waited his turn.

When his time was up, Kevin dropped into the pipe without any clear idea of what he wanted to do. He just wanted to pull off a couple of rad tricks. The first two passes across the flat bottom he was just fighting to stay on his board. He didn't come out above the lip at all and made a couple of frontside turns to gain speed. By the time he reached the frontside wall again, he was determined to stick a super-tough trick. He came up to the coping and ground out a stylin' Rock and Roll. Then he slipped back down fakie and started an invert, but couldn't roll his board over his head. Instead he came straight back down and crossed the well of the pipe fakie for a second time.

Kevin was quickly using up the space in the pipe but he was still determined to rock the pipe. He came up off the coping big and grabbed a honking Iguana Air.

Spectators yelled and applauded, and Kevin came out of the pipe feeling like he had just won a gold medal in the X Games.

He glanced at his watch and realized the snow mountain bike dual downhill was about to start. He knew his friends would kill him if he was late, especially since they had a mystery to solve.

"You're out of control, Jeff!" Jason yelled angrily.

"Don't ruin my run, man," Jeff shouted back. The two of them were standing at the top of the course for the snow mountain bike race. The crowd had backed away from them.

Kevin hurried over when he spotted them. Nat, Jamil, and Wall hadn't arrived yet.

"This isn't college anymore," Jason continued in a pained voice. "You cost that restaurant a lot of money. I don't mind you pulling stunts on me, but you can't do it to others."

Jeff stood there shaking his head. "Not me, man. Not me. I didn't do it."

Kevin stood to the side in shock.

"You don't have to lie to me, Jeff. But you should know, the police are involved," Jason said.

"You got the wrong guy," Jeff said. He picked up his

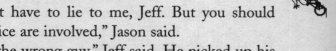

bike and slung it on his shoulder. "I've got to ride. I don't need this head trip."

Kevin couldn't understand why this argument was happening. Jeff and Jason were old friends. Didn't Jason trust Jeff not to lie to him?

The first round of the men's dual downhill was just beginning. The riders lined up to the side of the gate. The snow mountain bike dual downhill was a race down a mile-long course between two bikers. The one who won moved on to the next round. The races happened really fast—less than three minutes each. This year there were sixteen male and female competitors. That meant eight first round heats, followed by four, two, and the final. For riders that also meant there was no time to stand around and chat.

"Is everybody pumped?" the announcer shouted over the loudspeaker.

The crowd roared.

Kevin came up to Jason. "Are you okay?"

"I will be as soon as I get off this mountain," Jason replied. "I just can't understand why he'd lie to me."

"Maybe he didn't," Kevin suggested.

Jason ignored him. "Jeff should know I can read him like a book." He began to walk down the slope on the edge of the course.

The starting bell rang for the first heat. Two riders, both wearing skintight rubber suits, shot out of their gates, but the one in red quickly lost control on the first bonk. He augered headfirst into the packed snow. His bike continued down the slope flipping end over end, just missing the other rider.

Jason sighed and then tried to smile at Kevin. "Tell your friends to meet me at the store for dinner. I have tickets to tonight's party if you kids want to go," Jason said.

"Awesome!" Kevin replied. He couldn't help getting excited even though he knew Jason was still angry. "I love parties. First, Chase Johnson offers to coach me, and now we're going to an X Games party. This rocks!"

Jason tried to smile.

"Chase and I are like this." Kevin held up two crossed fingers.

Just then, Nat, Jamil, and Wall arrived from the slope above. Jamil was covered with snow.

"Hey, Kev! What are you so excited about?" Jamil called.

"We're going to a party tonight and Chase Johnson is going to give me some tips tomorrow." Kevin bounced on his toes. "Chase and I are like this." Again he held up his crossed fingers. He was so excited he felt like he was going to explode. "You look like a massive corn dog. What happened?"

Jamil grinned. "Just stress-testing my board with some radical tricks, dude."

"Yeah, like heading down the slope without falling," Nat cracked.

"Hey, don't reveal my secrets," Jamil shot back. "But more important, can Chase give me tips, too?"

"No way! He's my friend, not yours," Kevin replied. He wasn't about to share Chase with anyone.

"Who's winning?" Wall broke in.

"There's just been one heat so far," Kevin explained as he watched his friends unbuckle their snowboards. "Everett chundered, while Stephenson got a Sunday stroll to the next round."

The sides of the course continued to fill with spectators and photographers.

"Next up, Kirk Massey and Ryan Cutter. Kirk ranked number three on the NORBA Tour last year and Ryan won three Bear Claw Mountain Bike Races," the announcer said. "Both are primed for the dual downhill. They've been here for the past week working out the bugs in their technique."

Nat turned to her friends. "Do you remember Ryan last summer? He left everybody in the dust." Nat had worked at the Bear Claw races the previous summer.

A minute later the starting bell rang and the gates flew open. Massey and Cutter both had a great start. They charged down the hill like they'd been riding on snow and ice their whole lives. It was an incredible race that finished with Cutter nosing out Massey to win.

The crew could only see the beginning of the race. Then the course disappeared down the mountain.

"Next race will be Jeff and Lawson Tinter," said Nat.

"Did you get a chance to talk to Jeff?" Jamil asked.

Kevin shook his head. "But I did overhear Jason and Jeff shouting at each other about the prank when I came up. Jeff totally denied having anything to do with it."

"Then he's innocent," Nat blurted.

Kevin held up his hand. "I think you're right, but Jason says Jeff is lying. He says he's known Jeff long enough to know when he's lying. But it seems weird to me that Jeff would lie about something so important."

"Then who do we believe?" Jamil asked.

"Neither," Wall replied. "We keep investigating and prove for ourselves whether Jeff did it or not."

"The photos should help if they came out okay," Nat said.

Wall nodded. "We should compare them to Jeff's SUV."

"That would solve everything," Kevin commented.

"What next?" Jamil asked his friends as the last heat of the dual downhills left the gate.

"Photo store," Nat said.

Wall nodded.

Kevin had a map of the mountain open. He pointed to the terrain park which was just through the trees. "The skiboarding competition is just beginning. Let's check it out."

"Skiboarding?" Jamil said with disgust. "Why are you interested in that? I hear skiboarding just messes up the half pipe."

"Have you ever seen it?" Kevin challenged.

"Uh, no," Jamil admitted.

"Then don't dis it before you know what it's about. Besides it's a slopeside competition, not half pipe," Kevin replied. Slopeside competitions consisted of jumps, such as the classic snowboarding Big Air. "My dad has been selling a bunch of skiboards this winter."

"But what about the photos," Nat said impatiently. She dug her hands in her jacket pockets. "We've got to pick up the photos. The answer to the mystery might be in them."

"What's an hour going to hurt?" Kevin argued. "Let's just check out the skiboarders and then we can get the photos." He folded the map and put it in his pocket. "Besides, the guy at the store probably won't have them ready yet. He said he was really busy. Do you want to stand around and wait for that guy to get done? Wouldn't you rather watch some of the games than waste time cooling your heels in some photo store?" Kevin asked. He slipped his snowboard under his arm.

Nat exhaled a deep breath. A cloud of warmed air momentarily surrounded her head. "All right," she said with resignation.

The slopeside competition was just on the other side of a stand of trees about a hundred yards wide. The gang strapped on their snowboards and decided to go off-trail through the trees.

The trick to riding in the woods is not to look at the trees. Instead, a shredder has to focus on the spaces between the trees. This is incredibly difficult because one's eyes are naturally drawn to the trees.

Kevin entered the stand of trees first. Others had already used this route as a shortcut, so the snow was a little packed in parts. The problem with following someone else's line, though, is that it depends on that person having made good choices. This line wasn't the best. It was obvious the person hadn't done much off-trail boarding. The boarder cut too close to the trees and picked tighter, more dangerous routes. The closer someone gets to trees the greater the chance they have of slipping into a tree well. Tree wells are sinkholes encircling the trunk of a tree where the snow was unable to fall. If a skier or rider slides into one of these, he or she could drown in the snow.

Kevin moved in and out of the rider's tracks, which wasn't that easy in snow so deep. He leaned on his back foot to keep the nose of his board up. Then the nose could move out of the packed tracks and into the higher, deeper powder without his board getting buried. Unfortunately, riding this way sacrificed some control, and control is key when threading through trees.

Kevin swung his rear foot out to the side a little to slow his speed. He was coming up on the trees much too fast. As he slowed, he saw a clear path ahead. He carved uphill for a dozen feet and then turned his board into the chute. It was like riding on a mattress, soft and flat.

Nat, Jamil, and Wall followed Kevin's line. They all came out at the top of the slopeside competition.

Half of the skiboarding event was already over, but some of the top competitors were still to go.

The crew unstrapped their snowboards and made their way to a spot above the third jump in the course just in time. A skier came off the jump and hucked a 540 with both frontside and backside grabs to fakie.

"Awesome," Nat gasped. She had never seen a trick like that on skis, snowboard, skateboard, or in-line skates. "Now I understand why people are so stoked about these skis."

Next, the skier flew high off the jump, threw his right leg over his left, and went almost horizontal.

"Crash time!" Jamil called.

But Jamil was way wrong. At the last second the skier brought his right leg around and completed a 360 just before landing.

"Not!" Wall answered Jamil.

"How'd he do that?" Jamil asked.

"A burly late three-sixty cross-up," the announcer explained over the loudspeaker.

Before anyone could blink, the skier was off the next jump in a sitting position as he spun another 360.

"Yoda three-sixty!" the voice over the loudspeaker said.

The crowd went wild.

"That could never be done on a pair of skis," Kevin said. "I got to rent some of these."

"Me, too," Nat quickly said. She wasn't about to let Kevin get an edge on her in a new sport. "First thing tomorrow." She glanced at her watch. "But I can't wait any longer. I've got to see those photos."

"Okay, let's go." Kevin caved. "I got my look. Now we can take care of business."

The crowd broke into cheers.

"An awesome Misty Flip!" the announcer shouted into the mike.

Kevin backed away from the competition, afraid he might miss something, while knowing that he had a job to do.

Nat laid out the twenty-four newly developed photos on the carpeted floor of Ultimate Sports. "I still can't believe that guy hadn't even developed the roll when we got there."

"Give it a rest, Nat. He was busy, okay?" Kevin said. "We got the photos, so let's look at them and see if there's anything we didn't see before."

The four of them knelt on the floor and examined each photo carefully. They didn't find anything new.

"Well, the tire tracks came out good," Wall said. "Now all we have to do is start comparing the treads to actual trucks."

Kevin glanced out the window. It was already dark outside. "Let's do that first thing in the morning."

"Looking at every tire in town could take all year," Nat replied. "First we have to narrow the suspects."

"Narrow what suspects? All we have is one," Wall said, referring to Jeff.

"Okay, then lets check Jeff's car or truck," Kevin said.

At that moment, Jason locked the front door and turned off the display window light. "You kids ready for the party?"

"You bet!" Jamil said as he leaped up. "Let's go!"

"I bet Chase will be there," Kevin said. "He and I can hang."

"Aren't we good enough to hang with anymore?" Nat asked as she gathered up the photos and stuck them in a pocket of her backpack.

Everyone stood. Kevin ignored her.

"Hey, Jason. What kind of car does Jeff drive?" Kevin asked.

"A Ford Bronco," Jason answered. "And it's a beater, too."

"Do you still think Jeff is behind last night's pranks?" Nat asked.

Jason shrugged. "The more I think about it, the more I'm not sure." He went into the store room, grabbed his parka, and put it on. "But it's just the kind of joke he'd pull, at least on me, but probably not others." He looked at Kevin. "I'm kind of embarrassed about how I acted on the slope. I was a little too hard on Jeff."

The crew grabbed their jackets and followed Jason to the door.

"I just don't know. I guess I should believe him since he's a friend." He unlocked the front door and let everyone out. "But on the other hand . . ." He shook his head. "I just don't know. It's been about five years since I last saw him and I guess he could have changed, for the better or the worse. I just don't know."

That last comment caught the X-crew's attention. Was Jeff a righteous dude or a no-good dud?

At the X Games party Kevin spotted Chase Johnson and Gail Colvin sitting at a table. A half dozen other boarders were with them. Kevin ditched his friends and made a beeline for them. "Hey, guys." Kevin smiled and stood awkwardly at the edge of the table, hoping he'd be invited to sit down.

Chase looked up and nodded. Then he turned his back on Kevin and began talking to the guy sitting next to him.

Kevin stood there until he felt foolish. No one was speaking to him. Finally, he got the message that he wasn't going to be invited to sit. He turned and looked for his friends.

"What was that about?" Nat asked as she came up beside Kevin.

Kevin looked down at the floor, embarrassed. "I was just saying hi to Chase."

Nat had seen the whole thing. "Don't sweat Chase," she said. "He's just here to hang out with his friends."

Kevin nodded, unable to speak without betraying his feelings.

Jamil came over. "You won't believe this. See that guy with the TV camera?"

Kevin and Nat nodded.

"He thought I was a pro snowboarder. Is that cool or what?" Jamil beamed at the thought of being mistaken for a pro.

Wall brought sodas for everyone and the X-crew staked out a table by the stage. Three excellent bands were scheduled to play—The Debbies, Funk-Shun, and The Four Color Manual.

The first band, Funk-Shun, came up on the stage and almost blew out the sound system before they even started. A loud screech just about broke everyone's eardrums.

"Sorry, man," apologized Ed Bed, the lead singer.

Then Funk-Shun rolled into a gnarly rap about love, hate, and fast food.

Throughout the night, Jamil kept repeating, "I still can't believe he thought I was competing."

Kevin made a point of staying on the opposite side of the room from Chase. He definitely didn't want his friends to know that he had been dissed. He thought he had made friends with Chase and even bragged about it. He didn't think he could handle them knowing the truth.

As the party progressed, however, Nat, noticed something was wrong. "The party rocks. Why are you so down?"

"I must be tired," Kevin answered. "We should be going. It's getting late."

"There's going to be a drawing. Let's wait until after that," Nat suggested.

"All right." Kevin sighed. He sat at their table and watched the dancers in the middle of the floor. He saw Chase and Gail dancing by the stage and wondered if he should show up after the half pipe competition the next day. He might as well. Chase could show him a lot of cool stuff.

Toward the end of the party, the director of the games stood on the stage to announce the winners of the drawing.

"May I have everyone's attention, please? As you all know, everyone at the party tonight has been entered into a drawing for a one-hour free lesson with one of the top athletes in every sport at the games this year. This year there are six different sports featured—ice climbing, snowboarding, snow mountain biking, free skiing, ski-boarding, and snocross."

The audience applauded.

A woman carrying a giant fishbowl came up on the stage. The director reached into the bowl and pulled out a piece of paper. He unfolded it awkwardly as he held the mike in one hand.

There was a pause as the room went silent.

"The first winner of the night is Mike Sinclair," the director said.

The crowd cheered.

"And Mike will get a one-hour free lesson with ice climber Carrie Suttree," he continued over the noise.

The director reached into the bowl again. "The next winner is Dave Backus and he will get a lesson from free skier Carmen Orloff."

Dave Backus leaped into the air and ran up on the stage. He grabbed the mike. "I'm so stoked!"

Yelps and hoots erupted from the crowd.

The director took the mike back. "Next." He fished out another name and unfolded the piece of paper.

Everyone in the room held his or her breath as each waited for the next winner.

"The winner is Meg Ingols and she will get a lesson in snocross by the legendary Todd Hopkins!" The audience cheered. The director pulled out another name. "The next person will get a lesson with the awesome, fearless Jeff Fahey." The director unfolded the paper. "And the lucky winner is Kevin Schultz!"

"Agggghhh!" Kevin screamed. "I won! I won!" Kevin jumped up and down like a pogo stick. His hurt feelings completely disappeared. "I think I'm going to have a heart attack." He put his arms around Wall and Nat and squeezed hard. "This is my dream day." Kevin beamed. For a second he remembered how Chase had treated him earlier, but it no longer mattered. On Friday he was meeting Chase to get some half pipe tips, and then on Sunday he was getting an entire hour-long lesson with Jeff Fahey. The games ruled!

Kevin was so excited that had no idea who won after him. He was too stoked to pay attention. In fact, he barely noticed his friends leading him out of the party to go home. But in the back of his mind he worried that Chase would embarrass him and that somehow Jeff and Jason's fight would interfere with his lesson. This was all just too good. . . .

Outside the night air was frigid. The crew stuck close together as they walked up Elk Avenue. Kevin's dad and Jason had left the party early so Kevin had the key and was responsible for turning off the burglar alarm. He knew what to do since he did it all the time at his dad's store.

The street was well lit until they reached the block before Jason's store.

"That's weird. The streetlights are out on the entire block," Nat commented.

"Hmmm. I've seen one light out before. Once I saw two," Wall added, becoming suspicious. "But never an entire street."

Just then the growl of an engine filled the air. Around the far corner a rusted, old sport utility vehicle swung into view pushing a massive pile of snow.

"Let's get him," Kevin shouted as he and his friends ran up the avenue toward the SUV.

The SUV moved slowly and directly at Fashion Accents, a clothing store that had a big "Sale" sign across its window. Its headlights were off, making the SUV look more like a shadow than a real car.

The X-crew covered the space between them and the SUV quickly.

"Hey!" Wall shouted.

Suddenly, the SUV stopped. The small red glow of a cigarette stared angrily at them. Then the SUV backed up and swung around toward them.

"He must see us," Kevin gasped, out of breath.

The driver gunned the engine and threw it into gear. The SUV leaped forward, sending the snow in its plow down the avenue.

"Whoa!" Wall shouted. "Get out of the way." Wall spun and dove into a doorway.

Nat and Kevin followed, but Jamil slipped in the snow. When he looked up, the snow caught in the plow was coming right at him. Panicked, he couldn't move, but suddenly a hand clutched his collar and dragged him behind a tourist information booth.

By inches the SUV roared past them.

Jamil was afraid to open his eyes, but he cracked one and saw Kevin leaning over him. Kevin's hands rested on his knees as he tried to catch his breath.

"Thanks," Jamil said gratefully. If it weren't for Kevin, he would have been slush.

Kevin waved him off, unable to speak. Instead he watched the SUV lift its plow and drive over the mound of snow. Then the driver floored it and took off down the avenue.

Nat and Wall ran over.

"Did you get a look at him?" Nat asked her friends. "Was it Jeff?"

Kevin, Wall, and Jamil shook their heads.

"It was too dark," Kevin said. "That guy was smart to knock out the streetlights first."

"It could definitely be his," Jamil said. "It was a sports utility vehicle like Jason said Jeff had."

"Did anyone get the make? Was it a Bronco?" Kevin asked.

Everyone shook their heads.

"It was too dark," Wall replied. "Let's get back to the store. Maybe Jason can point out Jeff's SUV tomorrow."

"Good idea," Jamil said. He headed up the avenue toward Ultimate Sports.

"Wait!" Kevin shouted. He knelt beside the visitors' information booth where the SUV had scraped a large swath of the purple paint away. "This should make it easier to find the right SUV."

Nat, Jamil, and Wall examined the scratch.

"It's going to be hard to hide that," Nat added.

"Between the tire tracks and this, this guy is not going to get away," Wall said.

"Let's get a flashlight and the photos. We should compare these tracks to the others." Kevin dashed up the avenue with his friends following. Kevin's mood had taken a definite change for the positive now that the mystery was breaking.

Jamil held the flashlight over Kevin's shoulder as he laid down the photo next to the fresh tire tracks.

"Match!" Nat said quickly.

Kevin held up his hand. "Not so fast." He examined the major traits of each tread. After a couple of minutes, he said, "Nat's right. This is the same tire tread." He stood and handed the photo back to Nat.

"Then all we have to do is find the sports utility vehicle that has these tires and a purple scratch on its right fender," Wall said.

"I wish it was that simple," Kevin replied. "If it's Jeff's SUV, then this evidence will nail him. But since my gut tells me Jeff is innocent, we might have a lot of trouble tracking down the SUV."

"You're right," Jamil admitted. "There's a lot of sports utility vehicles in this town and most of them have plows on the front."

Kevin smiled. "Well, at least we have some real evidence now that ties the perp to the crime. Let's get to bed. We've got a big day tomorrow."

The X-crew walked back to Ultimate Sports. All the stores that lined the street were dark. As they passed a bookstore, Nat said, "I want stop in there tomorrow."

"What for?" Jamil asked. "You can get any book you want." Nat's parents owned a bookstore in Hoke Valley.

"To check out the competition," Nat explained. "I always like to see what other stores are doing. I think of myself as a spy."

"Okay, secret agent 007," Jamil cracked.

A few minutes later the team was out of the cold and burying themselves in their sleeping bags. But none of them fell asleep right away. The anticipation of the next day made each of them restless.

The morning came faster than anyone expected. Dawn light streamed through the window onto Kevin's face. He woke and rubbed his eyes.

Nat and Wall were already up and dressed. Jamil was still asleep.

Kevin wadded his sweater and threw it at Jamil to wake him.

"Ummm," Jamil mumbled. He pushed the sweater under his head for a pillow.

"Rise and shine!" Nat called to Jamil.

Jamil ignored her.

An evil grin spread across Nat's face. She snagged a water bottle and quickly tiptoed to Jamil's side. Chinese water torture. Very slowly she let one drop of water at a time fall onto Jamil's face.

At first he swatted at it like it was a fly. Then he rubbed his cheek.

Nat laid a droplet right on the tip of his nose.

Jamil shot up out of bed. "Whaaa?" He rubbed his nose furiously.

Everyone laughed.

As Jamil sat up, he looked at his friends laughing at him. "Don't make fun of the nose. The nose is sacred." He touched his hawklike nose again. Then he stood and kicked his sleeping bag into the corner. He pointed at his friends. "The nose knows."

Kevin and Jamil dressed quickly. Then they all went to the climbing wall while they waited for Jason and Kevin's dad.

Jamil tightened the harness and tied in to the rope. He glanced at the wall that rose twenty feet to the ceiling.

"Wish I had a little beta from Jason," Jamil muttered. This wall looked difficult. It was made of stone. The cracks and crevices were more like a mountain wall than the handholds of an indoor rock climbing wall.

Wall snapped the rope. "Move it, dude! I want to get on the wall today, too." He was belaying for Jamil, but he was impatient for his turn.

"Hey, I thought you hated heights," Kevin ribbed him.

"Not since I saved your butt on the wall last summer," Wall shot back. Before last summer Wall had been afraid of rock climbing, but he quickly got over it when Kevin was dangling thirty feet off the ground. Wall had to climb the wall to save his friend. Since then, he'd been working every week on the wall to overcome his fear.

Jamil made a two-tip squeeze on his first hold. Then he reached high with his left hand and jammed his fist in a crack. He smeared his right foot and found a firm toe-hold with his left. "I should've stretched first," Jamil said as he felt his muscles scream.

His knuckles burned when he pulled his hand out of the crack. He then crossed his left hand over his right and dynoed to a wide bucket hold that was just out of reach. His feet scrambled to get a purchase as he brought his right up to the hold beside the left.

This wall was built for grown-ups, so it offered an especially difficult challenge for Jamil, who was only five feet tall.

As he lifted his foot, his toe probed the wall until he found a small toehook. Jamil sucked in a deep breath. Then he scanned the wall above him for his next move. There was a pinch about a foot above his head that lead to a crimper.

"Here goes nothin'," Jamil said. He moved up the holds, but he couldn't find secure footing. He had to smear his feet against the wall and quickly barn-door three feet to his left to a safe, sturdy crag.

Spread out on the wall, he looked like a lizard scaling a rock. He moved slowly up like this for about ten feet.

"I'm going to blow you guys off the wall," Jamil called

down to his friends. Then he tried to deadpoint his next grab, and the wall spit him off.

"The wall will humble you every time you think you're the master," Kevin said.

Wall lowered Jamil to the ground.

At that moment, Kevin's dad and Jason arrived.

"Who wants breakfast?" Mr. Schultz called as he came in with several bags of food. "I've got bagels, egg sandwiches, juice . . ."

Kevin grabbed a bag out of his dad's hand and started rifling through it. "What, no cheeseburgers?"

Mr. Schultz laughed. "No, just healthy stuff like fried eggs and bacon," he replied sarcastically.

"That dad. He's a real card," Kevin replied.

"Very funny," Mr. Schultz said as he handed out food.

They sat in a circle in the middle of the store and ate in silence.

When Nat was done, she turned to Jason. "Where does Jeff park?"

"There should be a competitors' parking section at the slopes," Jason replied. "His SUV is a red Bronco with a license plate that says 'MANIAC.'"

"Maniac? No wonder you suspect him," Wall commented. He put his leftovers in the bag and tossed it in the trash can. "It's too bad we didn't see the license plate last night."

"Last night?" Jason said with surprise.

Wall explained what happened the night before.

"This is getting serious," Jason said thoughtfully.

"Yeah, it's not a game," Mr. Schultz said. "I'm not so sure I want you guys investigating this. It seems too dangerous."

"Don't worry, Dad," Kevin replied. "We can handle ourselves."

Mr. Schultz stood and threw his trash away. "Well, I want you to promise not to take any risks."

"We promise," the crew repeated together.

"Let's jet," Kevin suggested. "I don't want to waste my whole day checking out Jeff's SUV. I have to see the half pipe competition and Chase has promised to meet me afterward." He told his dad about having a date with Chase that afternoon and also about him winning a free lesson on Sunday.

"Hold up a sec, guys," Jason called to the crew. "It just occurred to me that every store that has been attacked was on the subcommittee to get the X Games in Crested Butte. The only committee members that haven't been attacked are the ski resort and the hotel," Jason said. "But if you think about it, those two members would be difficult to get at. If someone wants to get back at the committee, it makes sense to focus on the most vulnerable members."

A light went on in Kevin's head. "Do you mean that guy who came in here yesterday could be responsible?"

Jason laughed. "Not a chance, but it could be someone who is mad at us about bringing in the games."

"Is that all your committee does?" Nat asked.

"Well, not all, but mostly. We also make suggestions to the city council on ordinances on the marketplace," Jason explained. "But the big thing is bringing in the X Games."

"If it isn't Mr. English, would he know of anyone else who is that angry?" Wall asked.

"You got a point there," Jason admitted.

Jamil turned to his friends. "Let's check this out." He looked at Jason. "Where do you think we could find Mr. English?"

"At his office," Jason answered. He told them how to get to it.

Lugging their snowboards, the X-crew left the store at a dead run. They didn't want to waste any time.

On Elk Avenue, Nat stopped in front of the bookstore. "Wait up, guys. It'll just take a sec." She leaned her snowboard against the wall and disappeared into the bookstore.

The other three waited by the door.

"Listen, Jamil. You wait for Nat and check out Jeff's tires," Kevin said. "Wall and I will talk to Mr. English."

"No fair!" Jamil complained. "I should interview this English guy. You know I'm better at it." This was true. Jamil could draw people into a conversation better than the others. He was naturally gabby.

Kevin shrugged and looked at Wall.

"It's better if we split up," Wall broke in. "That way we don't waste the whole day on the investigation and we get to see some of the games."

"Besides, I've got to meet Chase after the half pipe

competition," Kevin said. "And no way do I want to be late."

"But you should wait for Nat," Jamil said to Wall.

"Oh, all right," Wall reluctantly agreed.

Kevin and Jamil took off down the street.

Nat entered the small bookstore. The store was empty except for the clerk behind the counter and one customer. Nat recognized him as the strange man who had been arrested the day before. The same kind of T-shirts they had seen in the police cruiser's trunk were piled on the counter.

Nat immediately scoped out the store. It was tiny compared to her parents' store. The shelves were stocked mostly with paperback mysteries and thrillers, the kinds of books vacationers like to read. Against one wall was a magazine rack that held almost as many magazines as there were books in the store. In another corner coloring books were stacked. There was also a large romance section.

Nat didn't see anything of interest, so she turned on her heels and started out the door.

But the sound of shouting stopped her.

"You can't do this to me," the man yelled. "I have rights."

"I'm sorry, Jeb," the clerk said, "but we just don't sell T-shirts."

The man pushed the T-shirts back in a paper grocery bag.

"Have you tried Fashion Accents?" the clerk asked.

The man ignored him and stormed out of the store. Stunned, Nat stood there for a minute.

"Sorry for the outburst," the clerk said to her. "Can I help you find something?"

Nat shook her head and exited.

Wall stood outside stomping his feet on the pavement and blowing his warm breath into his hands.

"Where's Kev and Jamil?" Nat asked. She glanced up and down the street looking for her friends.

"We decided to split up to save time," Wall explained. "They want to talk to Mr. English and we're supposed to find Jeff's SUV."

"I wanted to interview Mr. English," Nat said, disappointed. She picked up her snowboard.

"What can I say?" Wall said. "You don't want to waste the entire day on the investigation and miss out on the games, do you?"

"You're right," Nat grudgingly admitted.

"I wish we had left these at the store," Wall said lifting his snowboard.

"We can dump them at the lodge," Nat said. "Let's grab the shuttle to the slopes."

"Here it is," Kevin said as he stopped in front of a low brick building with a small parking lot in front of it. They crossed the lot and entered the building. They followed signs to the back where Mr. English's office was located.

The door was locked. Kevin knocked. They waited. No answer.

Jamil knocked.

Again, no answer.

"I guess he's not here." Jamil shrugged. The two of them walked out of the building. Just as they came down the steps, a beat-up sports utility vehicle pulled into the lot. It had a snowplow attached to the front end.

"That's Mr. English!" Kevin said surprised.

Mr. English pulled into an empty space right in front of them. "Hello, boys," he said as he got out of the car. "Are you looking for me? I'm sorry I'm late but I had to get my car serviced."

"Yes, sir," Jamil answered. "Jason told us you were opposed to the games being held here?"

"That's right," Mr. English answered warily. "Why do you ask?"

"We're investigating vandalism to several stores on the marketplace," Jamil began to explain.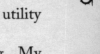

Kevin walked toward Mr. English's sports utility vehicle.

Mr. English laughed. "*You're* investigating. My word!"

Jamil got a little irritated. He didn't like being made fun of. "And the stores that have been targeted are owned by members of the committee that brought in the games."

Mr. English stopped laughing.

"We were wondering if you knew of anyone who was mad enough to do this," Jamil continued.

Mr. English stared at Jamil for a minute. "No," he

answered curtly. "Now, if you'll excuse me, I have work to do." He climbed the steps and disappeared through the door.

"That was strange," Jamil said to Kevin. "He sure did take off fast when we mentioned the games."

"Do you think he knows who's behind it?" Kevin asked.

"I don't know, but it sure is suspicious." Kevin and Jamil started across the parking lot.

Suddenly, Jamil froze. "Uh, Kev." He was pointing at Mr. English's SUV.

"What?"

"His tires," Jamil said. "They look brand-new."

"So?" Kevin replied.

"So, why is he getting brand-new snow tires in the middle of the winter?" Jamil asked. "Unless he wanted to get rid of his other tires."

"Are you thinking what I'm thinking?" Kevin asked.

"Has to be," Jamil said. "We better find Nat and Wall."

"But wait," Kevin called. He circled the SUV and examined it carefully. "I don't see any scrapes from the information booth."

"Maybe he cleaned them off, too," Jamil suggested.

They took off for the competitors' parking lot at the slopes.

Nat and Will jumped off the shuttle at the ski slope with all the other passengers. But instead of heading toward the lifts, they turned toward the parking lot after leaving their boards at the lodge.

In the lot several parking attendants stood in a group. They wore orange parkas and held red flags.

"Excuse me," Wall called to them.

One turned and walked over. "Yeah?"

"Where's the competitors' parking area?"

The girl pointed in the direction to their right. "Down there on the other side of the ski patrol building. You can't miss it."

"Thanks." Wall and Nat headed toward the patrol building and went around the back. A small parking lot, hidden from view, was on the other side.

The competitors' parking area was roped off and plastered with reserved signs.

Nat and Wall headed for an attendant who stood at the entrance with a clipboard in his hand.

"Sorry to bother you," Wall said as he approached. "But could you tell me if Jeff Fahey has arrived yet?"

The man glanced down at his clipboard. "Nope." He rifled through a couple of pages. "In fact, I don't expect him back. According to this note, he's windrawn from the speed event and left town."

"What?" Nat blurted. "That can't be true."

The attendant smiled. "Sorry, but it is. Better luck next time."

Nat and Wall quickly turned back to the lodge.

"We better find Kevin and Jamil," Wall said.

"I could watch riders in the half pipe all day long," Kevin said as he watched the top boarders warm up.

"The women's half pipe is first up, followed by the men's," the announcer said over the loudspeaker. "Get ready for the gnarliest show on earth!"

Kevin, Jamil, Nat, and Wall had found a spot on a rise about one hundred feet below the bottom of the pipe. The place was packed with spectators. This event was obviously the most popular at the games. The crowd was loud and wild and expecting an awesome show.

The first rider boned an excellent alley oop on the frontside wall with a backside 180 rotation. She worked the pipe effortlessly and ended with a monster McTwist that sent the crowd into hysterics.

Whoops erupted all over the hill.

"Chrissie's run is going to be hard to beat," the announcer said. "Next up, Midge Walters!"

Like a gunslinger, Midge dropped into the pipe. Her hands hung low on each side of the board, ready to move her board into any trick. She hucked a nice tailgrab on the frontside wall. Then she swung back and went big with an invert. Her board whipped over her heard like it was going to take flight. Then she brought it down just as fast and came down the backside wall like a rocket.

"Gnarly!" someone yelled.

"Burly Midge rocks the pipe!" the announcer said.

The rest of the competition continued for a couple of hours, each rider trying to top the previous one with monster tricks and rad style.

Once the women finished, the men were up. Chase Johnson led the men into the final round.

Kevin watched with a combination of excitement and embarrassment. He was excited to be hooking up with Chase after the competition today. But every time he thought of the previous night, he had a squirley feeling in his stomach. He thought maybe Chase dissed him because he was just a kid.

Today, Chase seemed to be on a mission. He came higher and burlier out of the pipe than any other rider. If he could keep this up on his final run, nobody would be able to touch him.

"Chase can't lose," Wall said.

The crew watched the other riders with a sense that the competition was already over. As they waited for Chase to drop in, the crew compared information on the mystery.

Nat explained that Jeff had withdrawn from the snow mountain bike speed competition and left town.

"Depending on when he left," Kevin replied, "that could eliminate him from our list of suspects."

"Unless he didn't actually leave until after the incident last night," contered Nat. "If we hadn't been there, no one would have known that he had come back to hit one more store."

"That's true," Kevin said. "Though there's still the problem with his motive. What reason could he have to attack these stores? And now that we think it could be someone who is against the X Games being here, it's even more unlikely that Jeff did it. I think we should focus on Mr. English." Kevin went on to tell Nat and Wall about Mr. English's behavior and his new snow tires.

Wall turned to Nat. "Could I see the photo of the tire treads again?"

Nat pulled the photo out of her pocket. "What for?"

Wall examined the photo. Then he gave it back to Nat and sighed. "I guess this isn't worth much now. We can't check Jeff's tires because he bailed, and we can't check Mr. English's because he put new tires on his SUV."

"Jason thought Mr. English was the least likely person to do it," Jamil said.

"But he also thought Jeff was responsible," Nat argued. "He didn't even believe Jeff when he denied doing it."

"That's true," Kevin conceded. "Either we trust Jason's opinions or we don't. I vote that we only rely on hard evidence to solve this mystery."

"Does anybody think it's over?" Wall asked. "I mean, we stopped the guy last night. Do you think he'll come back tonight to finish the job?"

Kevin smiled. "You're brilliant, dude. If he's determined to punish the committee members, he'll be back tonight. Let's stake out Fashion Accents this evening!"

"Great idea!" Jamil said. "But we've got to get help from Jason. We don't want to spend the night waiting in the street. We'll freeze."

"I bet he can get us in Fashion Accents for the night," Kevin said.

"Let's go!" Nat said. "We have a lot to do to set this up. We'll need flashlights, our sleeping bags . . ." She started ticking off the list.

"Hold on a sec," Kevin cried. "The pipe isn't even over yet. And I'm supposed to meet Chase afterwards."

Jamil smacked his forehead. "Let's wait for Chase's run. Then Kev can hang while we set up for tonight."

Just then, Chase Johnson dropped into the pipe. A hushed silence fell over the crowd.

Chase started with a quick toe grab. Then he shot through the well of the pipe and came up the backside wall. He planted his front hand on the lip, rotated 540 degrees in the opposite direction and landed riding forward.

"A monster McEgg!" the announcer said.

The crowd screamed. Nobody went that burly that high in the pipe.

Kevin got stoked watching Chase. He wanted to ride like him so bad it hurt.

Chase then came up the frontside wall and rose high out of the pipe. He spun a 360 and grabbed his tail late.

"Just another day at the office—with style!" the announcer shouted.

Kevin held his breath. He couldn't believe anyone could ride this large.

But Chase didn't know limits. He threw a beastly 900 and landed fakie.

"Air Chase!" the announcer commented.

He had just enough room in the pipe to pull off one more trick.

"It's got to be large," Kevin muttered.

This rad rider was in his own zone. He came up the wall riding fakie. It seemed like he had suddenly slowed down time. His board rose out of the pipe as he planted his back hand on the lip of the wall. Then he twisted like a pretzel and pulled a front flip, landing in the transition. When Chase stuck the landing, he raised his arms in triumph. Then he fell on his back.

"All right!" Kevin shouted.

"This guy is so awesome," Wall said. "I wish he was working with me."

Kevin smiled. He was so excited.

The crowd surged around Chase and lifted him onto their shoulders.

"Do we need to add up the scores?" the announcer shouted. "No way!"

When the score came up on the board, it was clear that they didn't.

Kevin stood at the edge of the crowd that surrounded Chase Johnson. Nat, Jamil, and Wall had already taken off to set everything up for that night.

Kevin tried to catch Chase's eye, but Chase didn't look his way. Instead, Chase made his way down to the lodge with a large group of people.

The spectators for the half pipe competition were streaming away to the next event, boardercross.

Kevin hesitated, not certain about what to do. Should he follow Chase or wait here? Chase said he'd meet him at the pipe. Or at least that's the way Kevin remembered it. So he hiked up to the top of the pipe and watched the workers strip the area of any evidence of the competition.

Riders were already in the pipe crossing back and forth, and endless series of grabs and airs were being pulled off.

Kevin sat on a mound of snow and laid his board on the ground beside him. His heart raced. He was both afraid of Chase coming up and talking to him and afraid that Chase would forget. The scene at the party the night before kept playing in his mind like an endless video loop.

After about twenty minutes, Chase still hadn't returned.

Kevin wondered whether Chase thought that since Kevin had won the lesson with Jeff, he didn't need to show up today. Chase probably didn't care that the lesson was in a totally different sport. But Kevin did care. No other sport compared to snowboarding.

Just then Kevin realized that if Jeff bailed on the dual downhill, then he'd bailed on the lesson, too. Kevin hadn't thought of it when Nat had said Jeff left because he was so distracted by the mystery. Now Kevin's lesson with Chase became even more important to him.

Finally, Kevin realized Chase wasn't going to come. After sitting and waiting for a few more minutes, Kevin screwed up the courage to look for him. He headed for the lodge.

He trudged down the hill and snaked through the crowd. Tents were set up all around by the sponsors of the games. People were checking out the latest equipment and snagging the free stuff.

Kevin spotted one company throwing bandannas to the crowd. He couldn't pass that up. So he elbowed his way in and held his hands up in the air.

"That's it!" shouted a guy from behind the table. "No more left!"

The crowd groaned. Kevin turned toward the steps of the lodge.

Just then, Jason was coming out of the building. He spotted Kevin. "Hey, Kev! How was the half pipe competition?"

"Awesome!"

"I wish I could have seen it. Have you seen Jeff?" Jason asked.

"Didn't you hear?" Kevin replied. "Jeff took off."

"What?" Jason said totally shocked.

"Yeah, he even withdrew from the dual speed," Kevin explained.

"When?" Jason stuttered.

"Last night I guess." Kevin shrugged. "When Nat checked the parking lot for his SUV, the attendant said he'd left for good."

Jason's shoulders slumped. "I guess I was too hard on him." He paused. "I just blew one of my best friendships. I should have handled it better."

"Well, we're not so sure he was behind the plowing," Kevin said.

"That would be great," he said exasperated. "I accuse my best friend of a prank that he didn't even do. And when he tells me he didn't do it, I don't believe him." He sat down on a bench by the steps. "He'll never forgive me."

"You were a little harsh," Kevin admitted, trying not to hurt Jason's feelings. "Maybe you can write him a letter." He gave Jason an encouraging smile.

"A lot of good that'll do," Jason sighed.

"We still need your help," Kevin said changing to subject. "We think the guy will strike again tonight and we want to set a trap." He explained their plan of hiding in Fashion Accents.

"Great idea," Jason said. "If we could catch this guy, that would be one success at least. It won't make up for being a jerk to my bud though." He ran a hand through his hair.

"Could you set it up?" Kevin asked.

Jason nodded. "I'll get on it now." He turned to catch the shuttle back to town.

Kevin watched him leave. Then he went into the lodge looking for Chase.

By the huge fireplace, he spotted Gail Colvin sitting on a couch sipping hot chocolate.

"Hey, Gail," Kevin said. "Have you seen Chase?"

She shrugged. "Who knows? He could be all the way to Canada by now. He's celebrating his win and that could last for days."

"Oh," Kevin replied. His heart sank. He was being dumped for the second day in a row.

"It gets a little boring after the fiftieth time, so I let him go berserk by himself and I get some riding in," Gail explained. She took a sip.

Kevin sat on the couch next to her. "Do you think he'll be back to meet me this afternoon like he promised?"

Gail laughed. "Not a chance. Maybe by Sunday, but don't bet on it."

Kevin and Gail sat silently for a couple of minutes. Then Kevin stood.

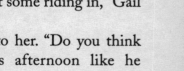

"Thanks, Gail," he said. "Later." Kevin exited the lodge and took the shuttle back to town. Chase was his favorite rider, but he was so rude. Kevin didn't think he could admire someone like that.

Past midnight, the X-crew sat in the window of Fashion Accents. Wind whistled up the avenue. Nobody was on the street and the streetlights were still out, so Elk Avenue was eerily dark and silent.

Kevin yawned. The day had taken a lot out of him and now it was way past his bedtime. "We should watch in shifts," Kevin suggested. "That way we can get some sleep."

"That's true. We don't all need to stay awake," Wall added. He untied his sleeping bag and rolled it out.

"I'm too nervous to sleep," Nat replied. "I'll wait up. You guys sleep." She had spent the later part of the afternoon and early evening getting everything together. There was no way she could go to sleep now. "Just be ready to put on your coats and boots."

"I'll hang with Nat," Jamil said. "Two of us should be up together. That way if one falls asleep the other can wake her."

81

Nat smirked. "I'm not the one who's going to fall asleep."

Jamil ignored her comment and picked up a hat in the window. "I'll pretend to be part of the window display." He made a dramatic pose with the hat held high like it was made of gold.

His friends laughed.

"Shhh," Jamil said. "Don't make me laugh." But he couldn't help it. He snorted and got hiccups.

Finally, Kevin and Wall bedded down and Nat and Jamil hunkered down for the long wait.

But they didn't have to wait long. Just like before, they heard the SUV before they saw it. The growl of the engine immediately woke Kevin and Wall.

"It's here?" Kevin asked.

The SUV came around the corner pushing a huge pile of snow. The avenue was empty. The street lights still had not been replaced. But to everyone's surprise, the SUV didn't turn toward Fashion Accents. Instead it turned up the other block and plowed the snow into the bookstore.

"Call 911! Call 911!" Nat shouted.

Kevin ran to the back of the store and dialed.

"Someone's plowing snow into the bookstore on Elk Avenue," he shouted into the phone. Then he dialed Jason's condo and woke Jason and his dad. When he finished, he ran back to the front and swung open the door. "They're on their way," he yelled.

His friends followed him into the cold as they pulled

on their jackets.

"We'll get him this time!" Jamil yelled.

They all dashed up the street, while the SUV pushed the snow against the front of the bookstore.

The X-crew reached the vehicle just as it was backing away to get more snow.

"Whoa!" Jamil cried as he slipped.

"Watch out!" Kevin yelled. The SUV was backing right toward Jamil. "Not again!"

Wall acted quickly and grabbed Jamil by the collar.

"That was too close," Jamil gasped. He put his hand on his heart and felt it beating furiously. He shivered, but not from the cold.

In the meantime, Nat had come up to the passenger door of the SUV. She grabbed the handle and opened it. "You're busted!"

The driver reached over and pushed her out. Nat tried to hold on, but what she grabbed came out with her.

As they watched the SUV take off down the street, a police car came from the opposite direction. It roared up the avenue.

The gang waved the cruiser over. "That's the guy!" they shouted as they pointed.

The cruiser flipped on its lights and peeled off down Elk Avenue.

"Hey!" Nat said when she realized she was still holding what came out of the SUV. It was a T-shirt, just like the one they saw in the trunk of the police car the other day. "This makes so much sense," she cried.

"What?" Kevin asked.

She showed the T-shirt to her friends. "This is the same shirt we saw when the police were arresting that guy selling T-shirts."

"So that guy must be the perp," Jamil said.

"That's right, and I saw him arguing with the clerk in the bookstore this morning. He was probably trying to get back at him," Nat explained. A wind whipped down the street.

"Let's get inside. I'm freezing," Jamil said.

"Where to?" Wall asked. "Ultimate Sports or back to Fashion Accents?"

"I locked the door to Fashion Accents when we left," Kevin said. "And I've still got the key to Jason's store. Let's head there. That's probably where Jason and Dad will go when they don't see us."

Jason and Mr. Schultz arrived at Ultimate Sports at the same time as the gang.

"What happened?" Mr. Schultz asked. He was wearing snow boots that weren't tied. His shirt was still unbuttoned, too.

Kevin explained the events of the last half hour. Nat showed them the T-shirt.

"Jeb Abair!" Jason slapped his forehead. "Why didn't I think of that before? This is just the kind of thing he'd do."

"What?" the X-crew exclaimed.

"Jeb's been trying to sell T-shirts and souvenirs on Elk Street ever since the games came to town," Jason explained. "We on the subcommittee turned down his permit. I remember his saying he was going to get back at us, but I just figured him for a nut. But why the bookstore? Its owner is not on the committee."

Nat nodded. "But this guy was in there this morning arguing with the clerk. I remember him threatening the guy for not carrying his T-shirts."

"So that means Jeff and Mr. English are innocent," Jamil said.

"That's right," Nat replied.

Mr. Schultz clapped his hands. "How about we all get some sleep? We can pick up the pieces in the morning."

Jason pulled some sleeping bags off a shelf. "You can pick up your bags from Fashion Accents in the morning. In the meantime use these."

Jason and Mr. Schultz left. The X-crew bedded down for the second time that night.

The bright afternoon sun splashed across the steep slope of the snow mountain bike course. A brisk, light breeze swept gently across the mountain.

"Do you think he'll show?" Kevin asked his friends as they waited at the top of the course. Uncertain whether Jeff would show or not, they had arrived early for Kevin's free lesson.

"I don't know, but I want to be here to see if he does," Nat replied. Her eyes scanned the slope for signs of Jeff.

"Well, the worst that can happen is he bails on me like Chase." Kevin shrugged. "And I got over that. I can do the same with Jeff."

"It'll just show that Jason wasn't a hundred percent wrong," Wall added. Wall knelt beside the bike Jason had let Kevin borrow. He was fiddling with the *derailleur*.

"Let's not wait," Kevin suggested. "He's not going to show." He grabbed the bike. "Who wants firsts?"

"Hey, wait!" Wall shouted. "He's here!"

Jeff suddenly appeared riding a snowmobile. He pulled up beside the X-crew. "What's up?" He grinned.

"We didn't think you'd show," Jamil blurted.

"When we heard you withdrew from the dual speed, we figured you left," Nat explained.

Jeff turned off the snowmobile and took off his helmet. "Not a chance. I promised to give you a lesson and that's what I'm going to do."

Kevin beamed.

"But I'm going to have to coach you from the top of the hill," he said as he limped over. "I twisted my knee and couldn't compete, so I drove over to meet a buddy in Central City."

"Are you okay?" Nat asked with concern.

"It'll take a couple of weeks to heal, but I'm fine," Jeff replied. "I'll be ready by the spring races."

"Great," Kevin exclaimed. He slipped his helmet on.

"Let's work on your start," Jeff suggested.

At the gate Kevin rolled his bike into position and hopped on. "Ready." He adjusted his goggles.

"First off. Getting a good start is key, but not crucial," Jeff explained. "The last thing you want to do is chunder, so it's better to be cautious when you're racing on snow and ice."

Kevin nodded.

"Now, what I want you to do is ride down to the first turn so I can see your technique," Jeff said.

Kevin ratcheted his pedal until it was in position.

Then Jeff opened the gate and Kevin powered down the hill. His front tire wobbled a little as it smashed through a clod of snow. Kevin dabbed his right foot and crouched low on the bike.

"Beautiful!" Jeff shouted.

Kevin picked up speed and crossed the twenty yards in a flash. As he came around the corner, he put his feet down and slid to a stop.

"You're a natural!" Jeff shouted.

Kevin waved and began to carry his bike back up the hill.

As they waited for Kevin, Nat turned to Jeff. "Have you talked to Jason?"

Jeff smiled. "Not yet."

"He feels really sorry for what he said," Nat continued.

"I know. I'm going to talk to him later," Jeff replied. "He's too important a friend to lose."

Nat nodded.

Jeff turned to Kevin who was just coming up. "That was great! I'll ride down to the middle part of the slope, and we'll work on that."

"Excellent!" Kevin replied.

"Give me ten minutes to get ready," Jeff said.

Jeff climbed back on the snowmobile and disappeared down the slope.

"I still can't believe he showed up," Kevin said. "After Chase ditched me, I figured it would be a total strikeout."

"Jeff's not like that," Nat said.

"How do you know?" Kevin asked.

"Jeff's cool," Jamil interrupted. "He's not a flake like Chase."

"He even said he's going to work it out with Jason," Nat added.

Kevin took his bike to the gate and stood there straddling the frame for a minute. Kevin thought about these last few days. He thought about how Chase had not kept his promise and how Jeff had, even though Jeff had more reason than anyone not to. And he thought about how he didn't have to worry about Nat, Jamil, or Wall keeping their word. He didn't have to think about trusting them. He just did. His friends would never let him down.

Kevin whooped and stomped down hard on the pedals.

"Go speed racer!" Wall shouted after his friend.

Kevin sailed down the slope with amazing precision and balance. He flew off bumps and cut a tight turn as he disappeared down the course.

"Let's meet him at the bottom," Nat suggested. The crew strapped into their boards and carved their way down the mountain.

XTREME LINGO

Auger: to meet the ground without meaning to, usually with the part of the body above the shoulders.

Barndoor: the result of a climber getting out of balance, causing the body to swing away from the wall like a barn door opening.

Beta: knowledge about the climbing route before starting the climb.

Bone: to straighten one or both legs during a trick.

Boned: a trick that's got extra style.

Bonk: the act of hitting an object with the snowboard.

Cab (Cabbalerial) while riding fakie, usually at the lip of a ramp, rider completes a 360 in the air and heads back down the ramp forward without grabbing. Named after Steve Cabbalero.

Chunder: to crash.

Corn Dog: when a rider is head-to-toe in dust, often after falling

Crimper: a small hold, just big enough for the fingertips.

Dab: touching your foot on the ground to keep your balance.

Deadpoint: a dynamic move where a climber lunges for a hold and hits it just at the highest point of the leap.

Dyno: a lunge for a faraway hold where a climber completely leaves the wall as he/she throws himself/herself up to the next hold.

Endo: to crash by going over the bike's handlebars. Short for end-over-end.

Fakie: riding backward.

Ho Ho: a two-handed handplant.

Half Pipe: a ramp that is shaped like a **U**.

Iguana Air: the rear hand grabs the toe edge near the tail.

Indy Air: a true "Indy Air" is performed backside with the rear hand grabbing between the feet on the toe edge while the rear leg is boned.

Invert: a trick where the head is beneath the board and the snowboarder balances on his/her hands.

Late: a term used to describe incorporating something into the trick just before its completed landing.

Lip: the top edge portion of the half pipe wall.

McEgg: an invert where the rider plants the front hand on the wall, rotates 540 degrees, and lands riding forward.

McTwist: an inverted aerial where the rider performs a 540 degree rotational flip.

Method: the front hand grabs the heel edge, both knees are bent, and the board is pulled over the head.

Misty Flip: a front flip with a 180 twist.

Pop Tart: airing from fakie to forward in the half pipe without rotation.

Rock and Roll: a lip trick where the athlete rides up a wall, balances on the lip with the board perpindicular to the coping and reenters the pipe without any rotation.

Stale Egg: an eggplant with a stalefish grab.

Yoda 360: assuming the Yoda Position in a spin.

Check out more rad lingo on ESPN's X Games website:
http://ESPN.SportsZone.com